No One Should Have Six Cats!

Modern Curriculum Press
BEGINNING
TO
READ
Series

MODERN CURRICULUM PRESS
Cleveland • Toronto

NO ONE
SHOULD
HAVE
SIX CATS!

Susan Mathias Smith

Illustrated by
Judith Friedman

Library of Congress Cataloging in Publication Data

Smith, Susan Mathias.
  No one should have six cats!

Summary: David's mother thinks he should give one of his six cats away, but which one should it be?
(1. Cats—Fiction)   I. Title.
PZ7.S65942No   (E)   82-2346   AACR2

ISBN 0-87895-988-2 Paperback
ISBN 0-87895-698-0 Hardbound

We have six cats at my house. But
soon that will change.

This morning my mom told me, "No one should have six cats, David."

I can tell that Mom thinks I should give one cat away. But which one? I love them all.

Herkie is cat number one. I found him in an alley one day. He had a hurt paw. He looked so sad and lonely.

Nobody knew where Herkie lived.

And nobody wanted him.

What could I do?

I had no choice.

I let him live with us.

9

Now Herkie's paw is all better. He can run and play and climb trees.

He and I are good friends.

I just can't give my Herkie away.

Zip is cat number two. She was sleeping near the bank on King Street when I found her.

Nobody knew where Zip lived.

And nobody wanted her.

What could I do?

I had no choice.

I let her live with us.

Zip doesn't do much except sleep and eat. But she's a happy cat. And whenever she's awake, she purrs.

I just can't give my Zip away.

Shadow is cat number three. I didn't find Shadow. He found me. One cold, snowy day he moved into our garage. There were some old newspapers stacked in a corner. Shadow used them as his bed.

Nobody knew where Shadow came from.

And nobody wanted him.

What else could I do?

I had no choice.

I let him live with us.

Shadow is afraid of most people. But he's not afraid of me. He lets me hold him close and pet him.

I just can't give my Shadow away.

17

Tinker is cat number four. She used to belong to my cousins. But last summer they had to move away. They couldn't take Tinker with them.

Nobody knew where Tinker would live.

And nobody wanted her.

What else could I do?

I had no choice.

I let her live with us.

19

Tinker sleeps under my bed. Every morning she licks my face and wakes me up.

I just can't give my Tinker away.

Boots is cat number five. I found him near the playground. He was just a kitten then. He was so little and afraid.

Nobody knew where Boots lived.

And nobody wanted him.

What could I do?

I had no choice.

I let him live with us.

Boots was too little to drink milk from a dish. So I fed him from a baby bottle. I saw him grow and grow. Now he is a big and beautiful cat.

I just can't give my Boots away.

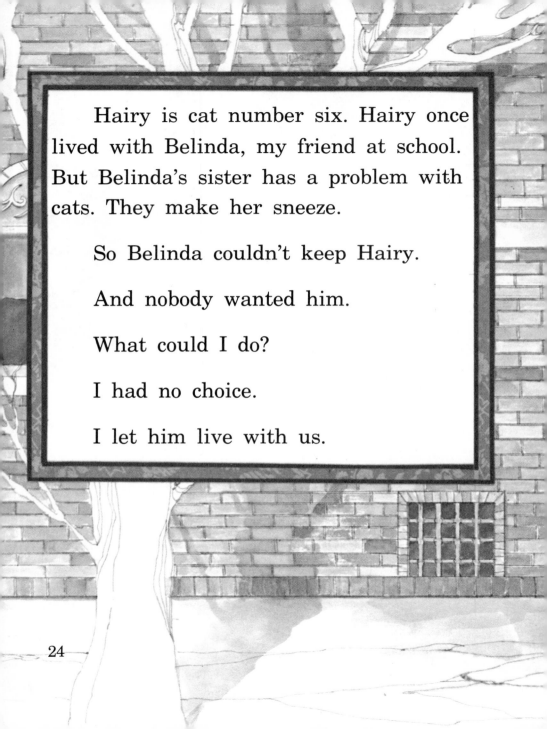

Hairy is cat number six. Hairy once lived with Belinda, my friend at school. But Belinda's sister has a problem with cats. They make her sneeze.

So Belinda couldn't keep Hairy.

And nobody wanted him.

What could I do?

I had no choice.

I let him live with us.

132

25

At first, Hairy did not like my other cats. He would tease them and get them angry. But now Hairy and the others play and have fun together.

I just can't give my Hairy away.

What will I do?

Here comes my mom home from work now. She will say, "No one should have six cats, David. Not even us."

But I don't know which cat I want to give away.

"Mom, what do you have?" I ask. "Is that a little kitten?"

"Yes," answers Mom. "I found her outside of the office. Nobody knew where she came from. And nobody wanted her. What could I do? I had no choice. I've decided to let her live with us."

"But, Mom, you told me that no one should have six cats. Not even us," I say.

"That's right," Mom tells me. "No
one should have six cats. Instead of
having six cats, we should have seven!"

Susan Mathias Smith is a free-lance writer and teaches English in a high school.

In addition to giving practice with words that most children will recognize, *No One Should Have Six Cats!* uses the 30 enrichment words listed below.

afraid	decided	newspapers	sneeze
alley		nobody	snowy
answers	except		stacked
awake		office	
	garage	outside	tease
belong			together
bottle	instead	playground	
		problem	whenever
choice	licks	purrs	
climb	lonely		
corner			
cousins	morning		